SOUNDS LIKE SCHOOL SPIRIT

words by MEG FLEMING pictures by LUCY RUTH CUMMINS

DIAL BOOKS FOR YOUNG READERS

For every special kiddo, ready for school to start.
And all the special teachers who fill the world with heart.
This is for YOU!
—M.F.

For Nate, and for school—a wonderful thing I most fully appreciated when it looked least like itself.
—L.R.C.

DIAL BOOKS FOR YOUNG READERS
An imprint of Penguin Random House LLC, New York
First published in the United States of America by Dial Books for Young Readers, an imprint of Penguin Random House LLC, 2021

Visit us online at penguinrandomhouse.com. Library of Congress Cataloging-in-Publication Data is available. Manufactured in China • ISBN 9780593108321
2 4 6 8 10 9 7 5 3 1
Design by Jennifer Kelly • Text set in Superclarendon • These illustrations were rendered in gouache, colored pencil, and brush marker, and then finished digitally.

Miss

We say BOOK, you say BAG . . .

We say NAME, you say TAG . . .

NAME! TAG!
NAME! TAG!

Raise your hands
and move your feet.
That's the spirit.
Find your seat.

Coat. Hook. Home. Base.
Seat. Spot. New place.

We say **DESK**, you say **CHAIR** . . .

DESK! CHAIR!
DESK! CHAIR!

We say CARPET, you say SQUARE . . .

CARPET! SQUARE!
CARPET! SQUARE!

Come on over. Hop in line. That's the spirit.
Circle time!

Say hi. Shake hands. Make friends. Big plans.

We say ALPHA, you say BET . . .

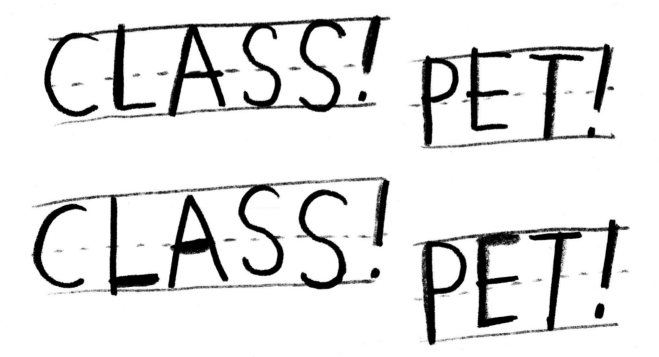

We say CLASS, you say PET . . .

CLASS! PET!

CLASS! PET!

Helping out
from A to Z.

That's the spirit.
1 – 2 – 3!

Read. Write.
Sing. Play.
Count. Share.
All day.

We say LUNCH, you say LINE . . .

We say SUN, you say SHINE . . .

SUN! SHINE! SUN! SHINE!

Taking turns and
standing tall.
That's the spirit.
Let's PLAY BALL.

Run. Slide. Jump. Chase.
Four square. Catch. Race.

We say PLUS, you say ONE . . .

We say EXTRA, you say FUN . . .

In the gym or on the bus.
That's the spirit. SIT WITH US!

Make room.
Here. Now.
Add. Join.
That's how!

We say LET'S,
you say HEAR IT . . .

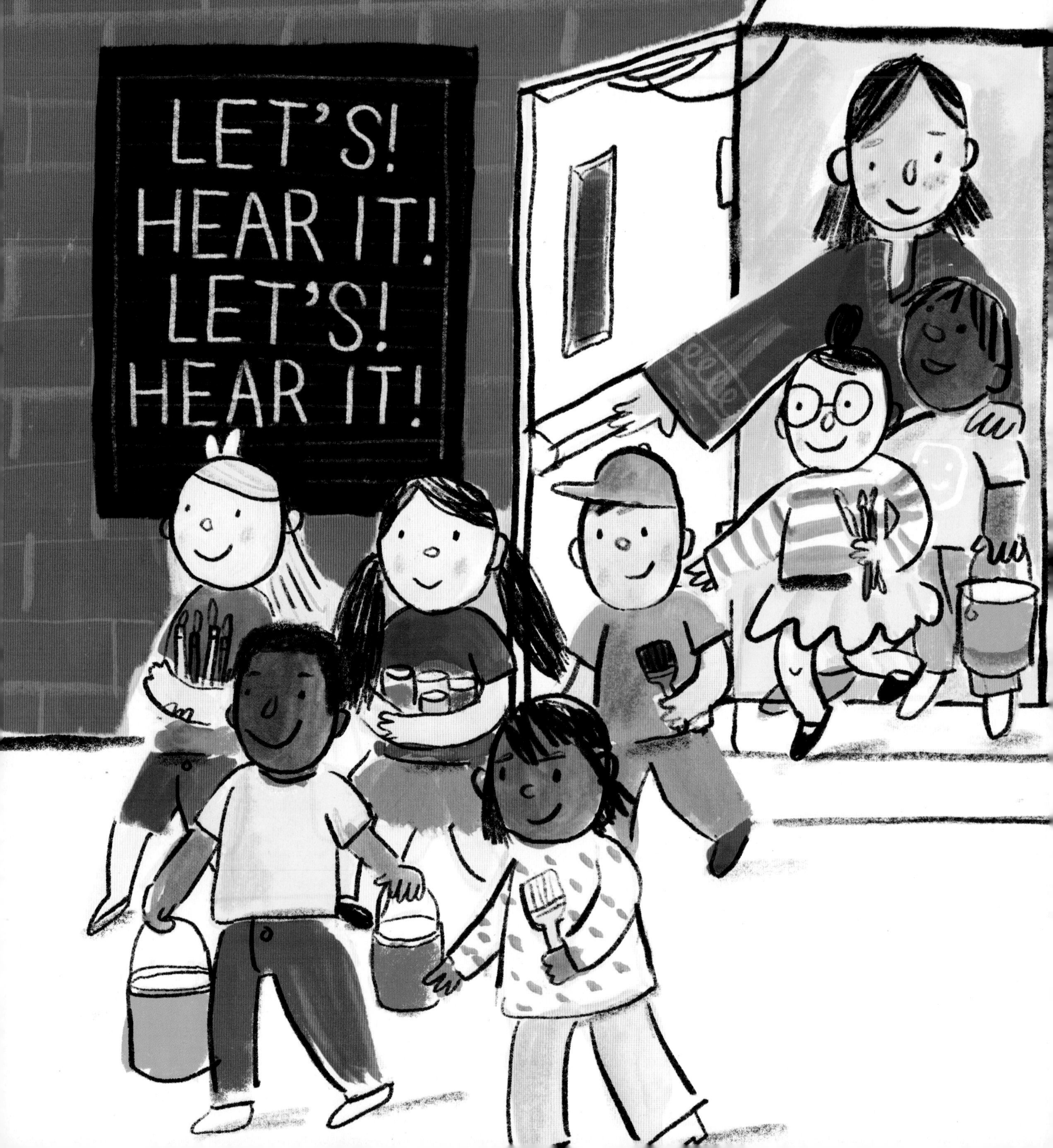
LET'S!
HEAR IT!
LET'S!
HEAR IT!

We say SCHOOL,
you say SPIRIT . . .

SCHOOL!
SPIRIT!
SCHOOL!
SPIRIT!

We can do it. We can dream.
All together . . .

L
E
G
O
T
E

IT'S
AMI!

Brains on.
Hands in.
Our school.

FOR
THE
WIN!

We've got class from

That's a promise . . .

friend
to
friend.